Galactic Treasure Hunt
Lost City of the Moon

Written by Jamie Childress

Illustrated by Chris Braun

Galactic Treasure Hunt – The Lost City of the Moon
Written by Jamie Childress
Illustrated by Chris Braun

ISBN: 1-931882-45-2

Printed in the United States of America

First Printing February 2005

Published by

Adventures Unlimited Press
One Adventure Place
Kempton, Illinois 60946 USA
auphq@frontiernet.net
www.adventuresunlimitedpress.com

For: Cameron, Finn, Kira and Hatcher

Without who's constant need for bedtime stories this book would not have been possible.

Special thanks to all of our friends and family for helping to make this possible.

About the Author – Jamie Childress:
When he's not writing stories Jamie Childress is an aerospace engineer who works for Boeing's "Phantom Works" research and development division. He's always wanted to go to the moon, and since NASA wouldn't take him, he figures his best chance to get there is with a space alien.

About the Illustrator – Chris Braun:
Chris works as a graphic illustrator for the Boeing Company. When he's not doing that he enjoys playing with his kids, karate, drawing and computer games.

Table of Contents

Galactic Treasure Hunt
Lost City of the Moon

Written by Jamie Childress

Illustrated by Chris Braun

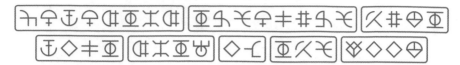

1. Backyard Campout

It all started on an ordinary summer night, in an ordinary neighborhood. The night was warm, too warm to stay in the stuffy old house on Stone Circle Court. So Jake and his little brother Scott asked if they could sleep in the back yard.

"Sure you can sleep out," said Mom. "You can sleep under the stars."

"You can use your new flashlights," said Dad, "but don't wander off."

"Thanks Mom, thanks Dad!" they both called

out as they ran about the house getting candy, comic books, drinks, and other camping gear that's critical for a summer's night in the backyard.

Mom tucked them into their sleeping bags on the grass, kissed them good night and said quietly, "Now Jake's the oldest, so he's in charge. Remember, if you need anything we're in the house."

"Mommm, we're not babies," said Jake, feeling very grown up, being in fourth grade and all.

"Yeah Mom," echoed Scott, being brave beyond his years as only a first grader can be. "We're big kids now!" And with that the boys snuggled down in their bags to look at the stars and shine their flashlights into the night.

2. The Spaceship

The evening was clear and still. The entire sky was nothing but a sea of stars, stars, stars, with hardly a spot of black between the twinkling lights.

"Look at those three stars," said Jake pointing to three stars all in a row directly above them. "Dad says that's Orion's belt, and the stars around it are in the shape of a hunter."

"I don't see a hunter," said Scott, "I just see a bunch of stars, and there are four stars in a row anyway."

"Don't be silly," said Jake, "Orion only has

4

three stars in his belt." He started to count them out loud, "One, two, three, uh four. Hey, where did that other star come from? It's not supposed to be there."

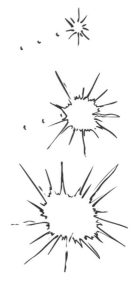

As the two boys watched, the fourth star started getting bigger, and bigger, and bigger. Soon it was the size of a marble, then a golf ball, and then a baseball. Very quickly they realized it wasn't a star at all, and it was coming straight at them!

"What is it?" whispered Scott.

"I don't know," Jake whispered back. "Maybe it's a spaceship."

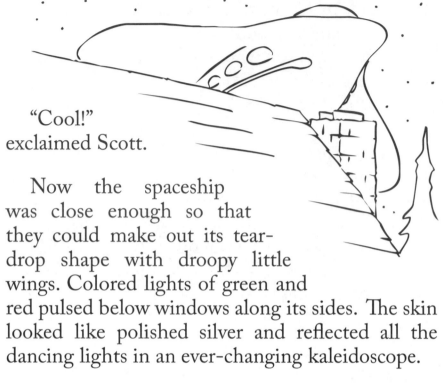

"Cool!"
exclaimed Scott.

Now the spaceship was close enough so that they could make out its teardrop shape with droopy little wings. Colored lights of green and red pulsed below windows along its sides. The skin looked like polished silver and reflected all the dancing lights in an ever-changing kaleidoscope.

It was still coming straight at them, but it was slowing down. It was so quiet, and so amazing, that they couldn't really tell how big it was, or how far away it was, until it passed right over their house. It was only a little smaller than the house, and it practically scraped off the top of the chimney as it passed over.

It made a soft rustling sound, like a gentle breeze through some leaves as it flew over the boys and moved past their yard to the woods just beyond. It slowly banked left, then right, and then left again, wandering over a patch of woods as if looking for something. Then it stopped in mid-air, and slowly dropped straight down into the trees.

"Aliens!" said both boys at the same time.

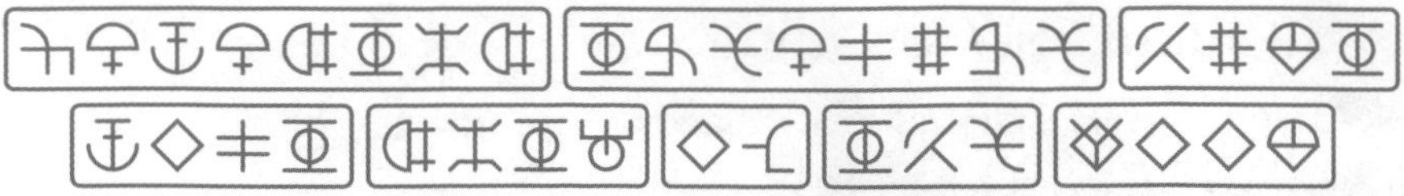

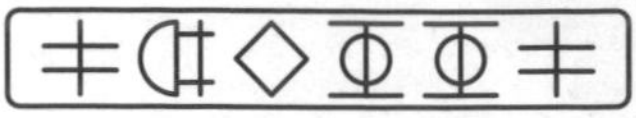

3. Spaceship Meadow

Jake and Scott were both talking in a jumble, "Did you see that?" "It was huge!" "It almost smashed into the house." "Wow." "Wait until our friends hear about this. They'll think it's so cool!"

When they stopped babbling for a moment, Jake announced, "We've got to check this out. We need to see where it landed. Then we can take the rest of the kids there tomorrow and show them."

"Dad said not to wander off," cautioned Scott, even as he got out of his sleeping bag and put on his shoes.

"We'll just take a peek," said Jake, picking up his backpack and turning on his flashlight.

"Do you think they're giant bug creatures?" asked Scott hopefully. "That would be so awesome to see a giant bug, with big bug eyes, and claws, and stuff."

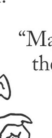

"Maybe they're bugs," said Jake nodding, "or maybe they're like dinosaur people or monster slugs. What if they're slimy?"

"Slugs? Yuck!" groaned Scott.

The two brothers hurried across the yard, and started down the well-worn path into the trees behind their house. There were lots of bushes in the way and forks in the trail, but that didn't slow them down because they knew the woods by heart. They went quickly towards the spot where the ship

9

went down. As they raced along, they shined their flashlights down the trail, looking for giant insect creatures, monster slugs, or any dinosaur-like shadows that might pop out of the trees.

After a few minutes they saw a blue glow ahead of them and they slowed down to creep up on the slowly pulsing light. There in the center of the meadow was the spaceship. It was just hovering there, a couple of feet off the ground. It slowly bobbed a few inches up and down, in rhythm with the pulsing of the blue light that surrounded it.

The boys were so mesmerized that they almost didn't notice a small ramp lowering down from the bottom of the ship and stop just inches from the ground. An alien stepped out onto the ramp and ran quickly down into the meadow.

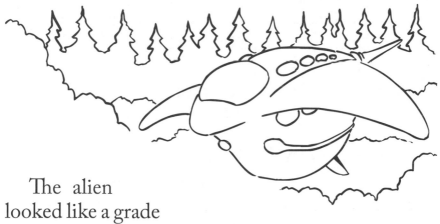

The alien looked like a grade school kid with a big bald head. He was dressed in shiny silver pants with big pockets on his belt and a light silver jacket. He was barely taller than Scott, and if they hadn't seen him run out of a spaceship they might have thought he was just a boy wearing a costume. The alien took one quick look around the clearing, and then headed into the forest, down a trail on the opposite side of the clearing from where Scott and Jake were hiding.

"Weird, it's not a bug, or a dinosaur, or anything like that," Jake whispered to Scott. Only Scott wasn't there! He'd already gone chasing after the little alien.

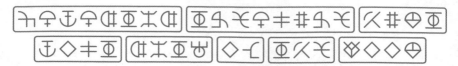

4. The Alien in the Woods

Jake called out in a loud whisper "Scott, wait up!" and quickly ran after his younger brother.

Jake caught Scott a little way down the trail.

"Turn off your flashlight," said Jake, as he switched off his own light and waited for Scott to turn off his. "We don't want him to see us."

Very quickly the trail came to another small meadow that the boys knew well. It was Stone Circle Meadow, named for the circle of stones in the middle of it. In the center of the circle of stones sat one square stone and standing next to it was the alien.

"What's he doing in Stone Circle Meadow?" Scott whispered into Jake's ear as they both crouched down behind a log where the trail came into the clearing.

"I don't know," said Jake. "Maybe there's something special about those rocks after all. Dad says they've been there forever, put there by Indians or something."

The boys watched as the alien pulled what appeared to be a small wand from his jacket and walked over to one of the little boulders that formed the circle. He touched the stone with the tip of the wand and the round rock rose up from the ground about a foot high and just floated there, looking like an odd-shaped balloon on a string. He then stepped over to the next stone and did the

13

same thing, until it too floated just above the grass. The alien went around the entire circle of stones until they all hovered above the meadow. He then stepped up to the single boulder at the center of the floating rocks and touched the top with his wand.

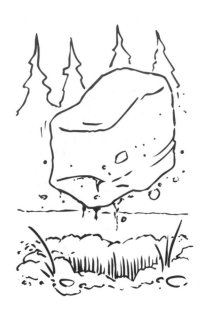

The rocks floating in a circle all started to glow in different colors. Some were red, some were green, some were yellow, and some were blue. Then they started to move, slowly at first, but gathering speed. Soon the glowing boulders were spinning in a giant circle around the center, going faster and faster until the colors blended into a rainbow of light. In the middle of that rainbow stood the alien looking down at the top of the center stone.

The boys were staring with wide eyes at the swirling scene just a few yards away when they felt the ground start to tremble beneath them. They heard a grinding sound coming from the center boulder and it started to rise as well, but instead of floating above the grass, it grew taller. More and more of the center stone rose from the earth and soon it towered over the alien standing next to it. As the tower rose from the ground, the boys could see strange writing on its side. The writing flickered with different colors as the light from the rainbow of rocks whizzed past each symbol.

The alien seemed to be reading the markings written on its sides and intently studied one of the symbols near the bottom. He then pressed his wand to the markings. A small door opened where he had touched the tower. The little creature seemed very pleased and did a happy dance, like a football player who had just scored a touchdown.

5. The Golden Sphere

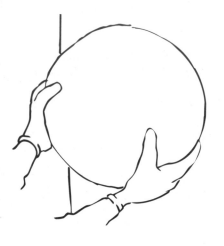

The alien put away his wand and then pulled a pair of gray gloves from his pocket and put them on. He reached into the hole in the tower and pulled out a polished golden sphere. Within moments the hole closed up and the tower started to slide back into the earth. The swirling circle of rocks slowed down and soon they all dropped back to the ground with a gentle thud.

"Did you see that?" Scott said with amazement in his voice as he ducked down behind the log and turned to Jake.

"That was unbelievable," agreed Jake, nodding at his

brother. "If someone told me he saw those rocks spinning around, I would have thought they were crazy."

"Yeah, it was like a merry-go-round of rocks," said Scott. "Did you see his magic wand? I wonder if he's a magician or something."

"He's a space alien. He doesn't need to use magic," explained Jake.

The brothers were so busy talking, they didn't notice that the little alien was hurrying back along the trail holding the golden ball and heading straight toward them.

Scott peeked over the log just as the alien was approaching. "Yikes!" he screamed and jumped up to run.

"Whaaaaa!" yelled the alien in response. Then he stumbled on the trail and sprawled flat on his face. The golden sphere flew out of his hands.

The sphere rolled right to where Scott was standing. Instinctively he knelt down and grabbed it. In an instant the ball lit up. Strange symbols flashed red and danced across the surface like they were on fire. Golden light-  ning crawled out of the ball and raced up Scott's arms. "Help!" he yelled and tried to drop the ball, but his hands were stuck to it and he couldn't let go.

Jake was already on his feet and rushing to his brother. "Drop it!" he yelled, grabbing the fiery ball himself and trying to peel it from Scott's hands.

As soon as Jake touched the ball his hands also stuck fast, and now they were both attached to the ball no mater how hard either boy pulled. There was nothing they could do but watch the golden electricity dance up their arms and then cover their bodies. It didn't hurt. The tentacles of light looked like they would burn, but they almost tickled. It felt as though hundreds of caterpillars were crawling up their skin.

When the light reached their heads fleeting images of space, strange creatures and fantastic cities flashed before their eyes. The two boys could hear distant music and strange voices speaking a sing-song language they'd never heard before. Even though they didn't understand the voices they

knew it was okay. The sphere was nothing to worry about.

After a few moments the music stopped and all of the golden lightning vanished. The ball dropped from the boys' hands and went dark.

6. Nojo the Alien

Both brothers were staring at the ball on the ground when they heard a voice behind them.

"Oh dear, dear. I'm terribly sorry. I hope you're not hurt."

They turned and there stood the space alien, barely three feet away. His head was big, too big for his little body. He had frog-eyes that were too big, even for his big head. A wide mouth, a tiny nose, and almost invisible ears, were set into his gray skin, and there wasn't a hair on his entire head.

As the boys stared, the froggy creature continued to ramble on as if nothing could be more normal than bumping into a space alien. "Well, you certainly

look all right," he said in a British accent, like a character in a Harry Potter movie. "We should get back to the ship, so I can have a proper look at you. Right then, off we go." He picked up the golden sphere and started down the trail towards his craft. When he realized after a couple of steps that Jake and Scott weren't following, he stopped and turned around.

"Forgive me," he said. "I'm being very rude. Here I am ordering you about, and I haven't even introduced myself."

He set down the sphere, walked up to Jake and stuck out a little gray hand with a thumb and three fingers. "My name is Nojolani, but my friends call me Nojo," he said in a happy tone.

Jake didn't quite know what to do, but he shook Nojo's hand anyway.

Nojo then turned to Scott and gave him a big smile. "You're the one who hopped out from behind the log, aren't you? You almost scared the poop out of me! I like that in a boy." He stuck out his three-fingered hand again and said, "Put her there."

Scott shook his hand, but didn't say a word.

"Cat got your tongues?" asked Nojo, his eyes gazing at them with the occasional blink of a transparent eyelid.

It was all pretty weird, but after a few seconds Jake spoke up. "I'm Jake, and this is my little brother Scott. Your spaceship flew right over our house."

"Are you a space alien?" asked Scott.

"No, I'm your long lost Aunt Petunia," he said with a laugh. "Of course I'm a space alien! I came in a spaceship didn't I? What else could I be?"

Scott rapidly lost all shyness with the little alien. "Do all space aliens talk so funny?"

Nojo chuckled, "I have to confess, that I learned English by watching all the Harry Potter movies about a hundred times each. I really love Dumbledore. Now, let's head back to the ship and I'll give you a tour. It'll be fascinating, I promise." And with that, Nojo picked up the golden sphere, and started down the trail.

For some strange reason it suddenly seemed very normal to be taking a stroll with a space alien

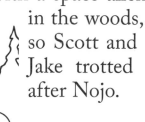

in the woods, so Scott and Jake trotted after Nojo.

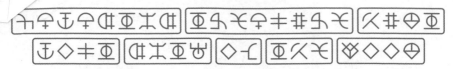

7. The Galactic Treasure Hunt

When they got to the ship, Scott and Jake followed Nojo up the little entry ramp into the spacecraft. They walked down a short hall that ended in a control room. There were several chairs scattered about, each with controls on the arms. There were video screens and windows on all the walls. Beneath the video screens were consoles with computer controls and lots of strange gadgets. The boys stared wide-eyed at everything.

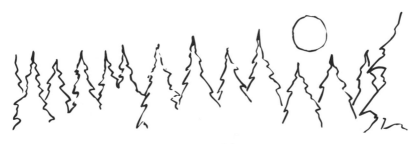

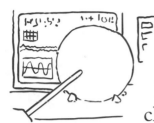

Nojo placed the sphere on a small table next to a computer screen and touched it with his little wand. When nothing changed on the computer screen Nojo looked puzzled, but after a moment he nodded to himself and smiled. Then Nojo turned the wand towards where Jake and Scott were standing and suddenly the computer flashed with unreadable symbols.

"I told you it would be fascinating," said Nojo, as he put his wand back in a belt pocket.

"Nojo, is this where you control the spaceship?" asked Jake.

"Yes, this is called the bridge deck," replied Nojo, "but this craft is more than just a spaceship, it's a

star ship. I come from another star, far, far away. I'm an Orion from a star called Bellatrix."

Scott piped up, "Hey, we know a constellation called Orion."

Nojo smiled, "I bet you do. Bellatrix is in the constellation Orion. We told your Greek ancestors that Orion was the name of those stars when we first came to Earth many years ago. Sometimes Orions come here on cruise ships for vacation or just to see the sights."

"Are you on vacation?" asked Jake.

"No, something even more fun—I'm on an adventure. I'm an archeologist," replied Nojo. "That's a big word archeologist, do you know what it means?"

"Sure," said Scott "Archeologists dig up old cities, lost treasure, and stuff like that."

Nojo laughed, "You've got it exactly right. You might say I'm on a galactic treasure hunt. I'm looking for lost treasure in a city on the moon."

"Hold it," protested Jake, "there aren't any cities on the moon."

"There are no human cities," responded Nojo "but there are alien cities. You don't see them because they're underground."

8. The Key Keepers

"Actually, there are two cities on the dark side of the moon," explained Nojo. With the wave of his hand a picture of the moon suddenly appeared on one of the view screens. "One of them is a very small and modern city. It's where we Orions stay when we're visiting earth. The other city is ancient beyond imagining. It was built by the Delphians so long ago that humans were still living in caves and even Orions were just simple people.

It was abandoned many thousands of years ago. That's why I'm in this solar system, to explore the remains of the Delphian's lost underground city."

"Do the Delphians have anything to do with that?" asked Jake, pointing to the golden sphere on the table.

"Right again! You two are very smart," Nojo said, a smile exploding on his little gray face. "That golden ball is a Delphian

key, or at least it was. I'm afraid that when you touched it, the computer keys that were in the ball went into you. Now you are the key keepers."

"Key keepers!" exclaimed Scott. "The key keepers of what?"

"Of treasure my boy!" said, Nojo with excitement in his voice. "The greatest treasure in the galaxy, the Pillar of Knowledge."

$E = MC^2$

"What's the Pillar of Knowledge?" asked Scott getting as excited as Nojo.

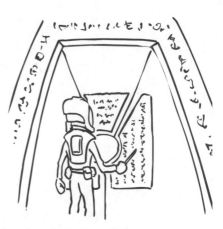

"It's like a giant library of all the Knowledge of the Delphians, who ruled the galaxy for millions of years," Nojo said, his transparent eyelids blinking frantically in excitement. "You see, I was exploring the lost city on the moon when I found a locked door. The writing on the door said that inside was a waypoint, which is sort of like a map to the Pillar of Knowledge." Suddenly, a picture of Nojo in a space suit appeared on the view screen. "Unfortunately, I couldn't open the door no matter what I tried. Finally I found one clue as to how to open the door. It was a riddle:

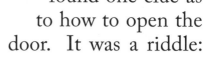

What goes 'round and 'round the center stone that's all alone, and should it ever stir, it's all a blur?"

"The stone circle!" yelled Scott enthusiastically.

"So there you have it," said Nojo. "The computer code keys to the greatest treasure in the galaxy were in your backyard and now they are in you. Unfortunately, the sphere is now useless, so now you're the only ones who can open that door."

"But the door is on the moon," said Jake, with wonder in his voice.

"So, what do you say, anyone interested in a quick trip to the moon?" asked Nojo. "We can be there before you know it."

Jake and Scott looked at each other and both burst out at the same time with a big, "All right!"

9. Blast off

Nojo sat down in a chair in front of the main screen and pointed to the two chairs on either side of him. "You guys can sit here, so you can see everything," he suggested.

"Where's the seat belt?" asked Scott, as he and Jake sat down.

"There aren't any seat belts," said Nojo. "Trust me, you won't need them."

"Are we going to do a countdown?" asked Jake.

"I don't normally," said Nojo, "but we can if you'd like to."

"Three, two, one, blast off!" yelled Scott.

Nojo pressed a button on the console in front of him and pulled upward gently on a joystick. The

ship rose slowly and si-
lently into the sky until
it cleared the trees. They
could see all directions
around the ship on the moni-
tors and windows that wrapped
around the control room.

"Look, there's our house!" exclaimed
Jake, as the craft rose ever higher.

"And our school," said Scott looking
through the monitor on the right. "Can
we buzz the schoolyard?"

"You bet! There's nothing I like better than a good buzzing," said Nojo as
the craft banked right and swooped
towards the school at high speed.

Scott and Jake grabbed their
armrests expecting to get
thrown around as the

ship banked and accelerated, but they soon discovered that they didn't feel the ship turn or speed up at all. Though they could see they were zipping toward the school faster and faster, it felt more like they were sitting in a chair in their living room and just watching a show on TV.

Nojo laughed as he watched them relax their grip on the chairs. "I told you that you didn't need seat belts. This starship uses electro-gravity for propulsion. We're in a gravity-bubble, so no matter how fast we go, or how quickly we turn, you'll always feel like you're just sitting on your couch at home."

"Our friends will never believe this," said Scott.

"They will if we leave a mark at the school," said Jake. "Nojo, could we write our names on the front steps with a laser or something?"

"Hum," said Nojo, "I'm not sure that's such a good idea. It would be hard to erase and they might get

36

mad. How about we just leave them a little present in the soccer field."

Nojo banked sharply and flew just a few feet over the grassy soccer field. The grass turned yellow wherever he went. He zigged and zagged and spiraled the ship around and around until he had turned the whole field into a giant maze.

"Let them try to explain that," he said with a chuckle, and pulled up steeply into the night sky.

Just as the ship was rising high above the town, a voice crackled out of a speaker in the computer console. *"Roger that intercept control. I have the bogey on radar at flight level two-zero and climbing, range twenty miles. Will close with target for visual. Eagle-One out."*

Nojo's eyes lit up with excitement. "Boys, you're in for a real treat. It seems we've attracted the attention of your Air Force. I do love a good chase!"

10. Bogey On Our Six

Nojo pushed a button. In the lower corner of the front screen a picture popped up with an overhead view of the town. It was like looking down on everything from a balloon floating high up in the sky.

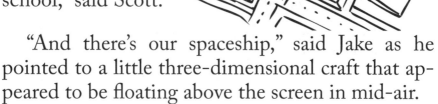

"Hey, I see the school," said Scott.

"And there's our spaceship," said Jake as he pointed to a little three-dimensional craft that appeared to be floating above the screen in mid-air.

"What are those?" asked Scott, pointing to a tiny pair of aircraft approaching the town from the top of the picture.

"I know," said Jake proudly. "Those are F-15 Eagle fighter jets."

"Right you are young man," said Nojo, obviously pleased that Jake knew the aircraft's name. "Those fighters were scrambled from

the air base north of here when I came in to land. I figured they'd come to see if they could catch me. They always try, but they haven't caught me yet."

Then Nojo winked a transparent eyelid at them, banked the ship and headed straight toward the oncoming Eagle fighters. "Let's give them a show," he said, "tally ho!"

The pilot's voice crackled again over the radio. *Eagle-One has bogey approaching at high speed. I*

*have an
unknown aircraft
type on visual. It appears to be a UFO!"*

"Fighters twelve-o-clock!" yelled Jake, pointing at the blinking wing lights of approaching F-15s on the screen in front of him. "I heard that in a movie once," he explained. "It's like the numbers on a clock. Twelve-o-clock means they're right in front of us, and six-o-clock means they're behind us."

"Well they won't be at twelve-o-clock for long," said Nojo as the star-ship rocketed past the two approaching jets so fast that the aircraft were a blur.

"What the heck was that??!!" came the voice over the radio. *"Intercept control, intercept control, bogey is on our six. Repeat, Eagle-One has bogey on our six, moving at extreme speed."*

Just after they passed the two F-15s, Nojo stopped the spaceship and held it hovering in the sky. Jake and Scott turned in their seats so they could more easily watch the fighters race away.

"I love airplanes," said Nojo. "They're so graceful, even if they do use old-fashioned wings and jet engines. Someday your people will discover anti-gravity, but for now we can enjoy watching these fine antiques."

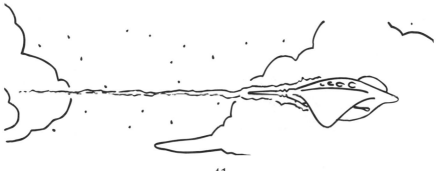

A new voice came over the radio. *"Eagle-One, this is intercept control. The UFO has stopped directly on your six-o-clock. You are to engage bogey. Weapons release authorized!"*

"Roger that!" replied Eagle-One.

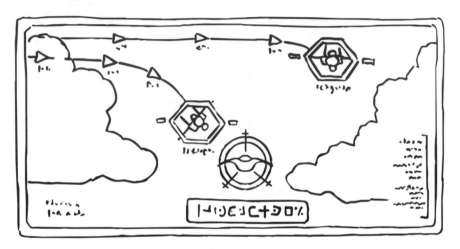

"I'll switch the view screens to night-vision, so we can see them better," said Nojo as the windows turned green and the F-15 aircraft became suddenly visible, as if it were daytime.

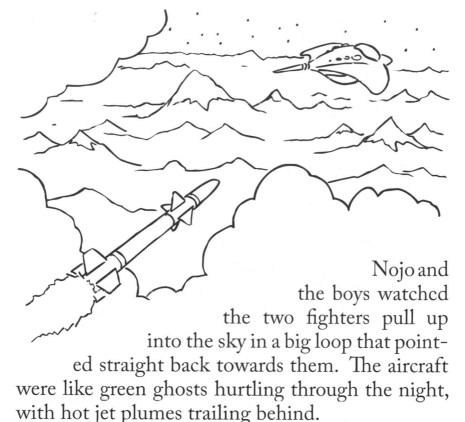

Nojo and
the boys watched
the two fighters pull up
into the sky in a big loop that pointed straight back towards them. The aircraft
were like green ghosts hurtling through the night,
with hot jet plumes trailing behind.

"Radar is locked," announced Eagle-One calmly.
"Fox one, fox two. Missiles away."

Suddenly two brilliant points of light raced away
from the lead fighter jet. The two missiles were
headed straight toward the starship.

⟨𝄢𝄢𝄢𝄢⟩

11. Into Outer Space

"They're shooting at us!" yelled Scott.

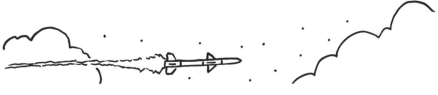

"Yes, of course," replied Nojo very matter-of-factly. "They always do that. You'd think they'd learn, but they never seem to. Sometimes it makes me wonder if they ever talk to one another."

"We've got to get out of here—they're shooting at US!" yelled Scott again, pointing to the missiles growing larger every second on the screen.

"What do you say Jake, should we get out of here?" Nojo asked, giving Jake a wink and a nod.

"Good idea!" Jake agreed instantly, while trying to sound cool and unconcerned.

"Then press that button right there," said Nojo, pointing to a round red button on the computer console.

"You mean that one?" asked Jake nervously, with the missiles just seconds away.

"That's the one," said Nojo "Best to do it soon lad, or we just might go kablooiiee."

"Press the button!" screamed Scott.

So Jake pressed the button, with not a second to spare.

The spacecraft shot straight up so fast that, from the ground, it must have looked like they had just vanished into thin air. Both missiles passed harmlessly beneath them as they zoomed into space.

"Wahoooo, wahooo!" The boys were yelling so loudly at having escaped the missiles that they hardly noticed the earth falling away below them.

"Hey," said Jake when he finally stopped whooping. "We're in outer space."

"Yes indeed! You two are now officially astronauts," said Nojo with great fanfare. "All right then, as official astronauts, can you tell me what that is?" he asked, pointing at what looked like a collection of tinker toys and tin cans floating above the Earth.

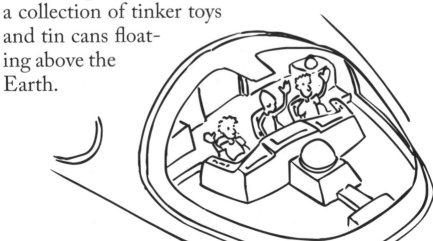

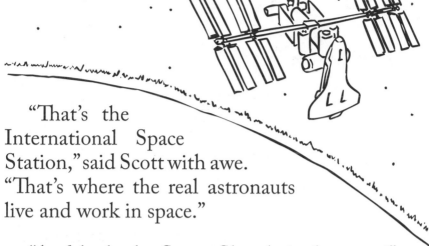

"That's the International Space Station," said Scott with awe. "That's where the real astronauts live and work in space."

"And look, the Space Shuttle is there too!" said Jake, pointing to where the shuttle was docked to the Space Station.

Just then, one of the Space Station astronauts looked out a window and saw them as they flew past. Nojo and the boys all waved. The astronaut's jaw dropped, her eyes went wide, then shyly she waved back as they flew away.

12. Earth to the Moon

The boys looked down from the ship and watched entire oceans and continents pass below them in a couple of quick heartbeats. The lights of the cities twinkled on the part of earth that was in night, and a lightning storm lit up the sea. As they got further from Earth, the sun peeked around the corner of the giant blue and brown sphere. Suddenly the rim of the atmosphere sparkled brilliant yellow with a ring of golden sunlight. Jake thought it was a sight more magical than the finest trick a wizard ever dreamed of.

Nojo banked the ship toward the moon and the boys turned around in their seats to watch the Earth grow smaller and smaller in the view screen

at the rear of the bridge deck. Soon it no longer filled the entire screen and they could see it now as a giant multi-colored ball. Earth was floating in a vast sea of blackness filled with zillions of stars. Each star was a sun, just like our sun, only far, far away.

Scott looked at the stars surrounding the earth and asked Nojo, "Is one of those stars your star?"

"My home of Bellatrix is that one," said Nojo pointing to a bright star just above the three stars in Orion's belt. "It's a giant sun, much larger than your sun. It only looks small from here because it's more than two hundred light years away. Do you know what a light year is?"

"Sure," said Jake, "I learned that in science last year. It's how far a beam of light can go in one year. A light year is a really long way. It's like going from Earth to Pluto and back a thousand times."

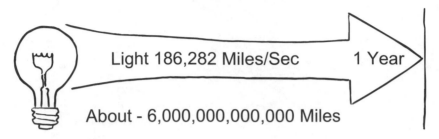

Light 186,282 Miles/Sec   1 Year

About - 6,000,000,000,000 Miles

"It must have taken a really long time to get here," said Scott. "I bet it was really boring. I hate even driving to grandma's house and that only takes a day."

"Actually it didn't take as long as you might think. This is a star ship after all—it can go pretty fast when I want it to!" Nojo said with a sly grin. "In fact, we've just been puttering along in first gear and we're already at the moon."

The boys were so enthralled watching the view of the stars, and the Earth get smaller, that they hadn't even noticed the moon growing large before them in the forward view screen.

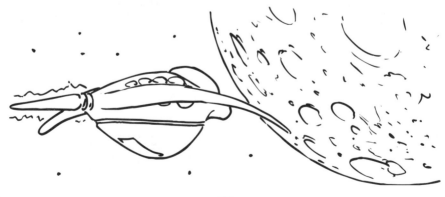

"Wooow, cool!" exclaimed both boys in unison, turning around and staring in disbelief as they went into orbit around the moon.

"Jake, you want to try driving this baby?" asked Nojo.

"You mean fly a starship? Ahhhh… yeah… sure!" stammered Jake. "What do I do?"

"It's very simple," said Nojo pointing to Jake's controls. "Grab the joystick on your chair and wherever you point the joystick, that's where you'll go. The harder you push, the faster you'll get there. Take us to the dark side of the moon. That's where the lost city is located."

"You got it!" whooped Jake, as he took the joystick and banked the ship towards the far side of the moon, feeling nervous, excited, and in utter disbelief all at the same time. An hour ago he was in his back yard and now he was flying a star ship. It was unreal.

13. Jake Flies a Star Ship

Jake couldn't wait to put this baby through its paces. He experimented with the joystick, flying the ship like it was a giant videogame. The craft was so nimble it responded in the blink of an eye to every twitch of Jake's hand. The more he played with the controls, the more confident and excited he got. His eyes flickered and a wide grin spread across his face. It was the biggest rush he'd ever felt in his life.

When he was sure he'd mastered the controls, he pushed the joystick forward and watched the stark landscape of the moon flash beneath the spaceship at ever-increasing speed. The surface of the moon was a harsh place. With no atmosphere to soften the sun's light, 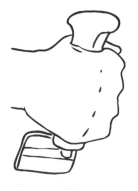 everything was in black and white, with no reds, or greens, or blues, or any other colors of the rainbow.

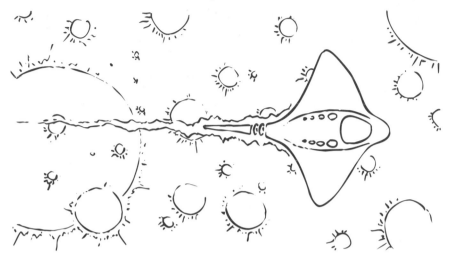

It was like looking down on a coloring book before anyone had a chance to color it in.

"So, where exactly is this lost city?" asked Jake, still banking and cranking just for fun. "I don't see anything down there but craters and mountains."

"It's just there, on the left," replied Nojo, pointing to a crater in the distance. "See the small crater, just behind those mountains?"

Scott piped up, "I see the crater, but I still don't see any city."

"Ah yes, that's the tricky part isn't it," replied Nojo. "It doesn't look much like a city does it? But what you don't know is that it's not a crater at all. It's really

a giant
spaceport
built like a stadium.
The doors to the under-
ground city are all around the
inside edge of the crater. Take us
down Jake and you'll see."

"Let's rock and roll!" shouted Jake, while
banking just a hair left and pushing the nose of
the star ship toward the mountains.

Jake worked the joystick with amazing
skill, bringing the speedy ship down
until the surface of the moon was
so close you could clearly see

individual stones in the dust. He then pulled them level with a snap of his wrist at the last moment. The maneuver was so fast that Nojo gasped as they rocketed past a crater rim barely five feet below the belly of the ship. Jake was headed straight for the jagged wall of rock Nojo had pointed to a moment earlier.

Nojo cleared his throat loudly. "Umm Jake, don't you think you could go just a bit higher?"

"Don't worry, Nojo," came Jake's confident reply as he made a minor adjustment to keep them from slamming into a boulder. "I've got the highest score in the whole school on the OuterWorld Race game. I never crash. Well, almost never anyway."

"Almost never?" repeated Nojo with alarm.

There was no time for chitchatting, since they were on the mountains in two heartbeats. The peaks looked like the teeth of a giant dragon and Jake was taking the ship right down its throat. "Yeee haaww!" hollered Jake, pulling back on the stick and banking hard. The star ship shot up through a narrow gap between two sparkling towers of rock and flashed out the far side.

"That was cool!" said Scott energetically, giving Jake a high five. "Hey Nojo, when do I get to drive?"

"When I recover from letting Jake drive, which will be in about a hundred years," replied Nojo with a groan as he slowly pulled his hands away from his eyes and peeked at the forward view screen. They were slowly circling above the small crater as Jake spiraled down over the lost city of the moon.

14. Lost City of the Moon

"Nojo, you're right," said Jake excitedly, "the sides of the crater look like walls and there's lots of doors. Which one should I pick?"

"There," said Nojo, pointing to an open door that was right in front of them. "The open door leads right into the chamber where the waypoint should be. It's a big door, so you ought to be able to fly the ship right into the chamber. Now, no flashy flying. I don't think my heart can take it."

"No problem," replied Jake.

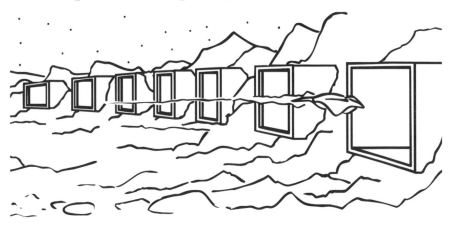

Jake flew the spaceship toward the entrance and soon they could see just how gigantic it really was. The door in the side of the crater was large enough to fly a jumbo jet through. Jake had no trouble sliding the craft into the cavernous interior. Jake was expecting it to be dark inside, but the walls seemed to glow with soft yellow light, making it easy to see. Once inside, they found themselves in a vast hangar with several hallways dead ahead.

"Set it down nice and gentle next to the hallway on the left, if you please," instructed Nojo.

"Soft as a feather," replied Jake, bringing the craft to a stop in front of the hallway entrance and then slowly taking it down until they hovered just off the floor.

"All right then, time to get suited up," said Nojo as he got out of his chair and walked to the back of the bridge deck.

"Suited up for what?" asked Scott.

"To take a walk on the moon, of course," said Nojo, just as he stepped onto a small platform and pressed a button on the wall. The platform began to glow as bright waves of energy danced and crawled up Nojo, scanning his body from his feet to his head. A shiny silver space suit and helmet rapidly appeared as if it were being knitted around him out of thin air.

"That's a neat trick!" exclaimed Scott. "How did you do that?"

"It's called nano-technology," said Nojo. "The computer takes your measurements and then builds the suit out of atoms around you. It's pretty handy really. You can use it to make just about anything, as long as you have it programmed into the computer."

"Do you have the new Action-Max doll programmed in?" asked Scott hopefully. "Mine broke last week."

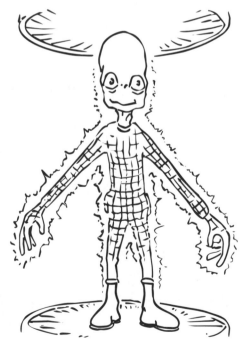

"I don't think so," said Nojo with a little giggle, "but step right up and I'll bet we can make a spacesuit just your size. We'll have to wear spacesuits here—this part of the ancient city isn't sealed anymore, so there isn't any air, and it's very cold."

In just a few minutes the nano-technology machine made spacesuits for both Jake and Scott. The helmets had large clear visors that wrapped around their faces and radios so they could talk to each other. The fabric of the one-piece suits fit close to their bodies, even covering their feet and hands with built-in boots and gloves. A belt around their waist held their air supply and a heater to keep them warm.

"Now that you're all suited up, just step into the airlock and we're off," said Nojo, his voice a tiny bit crackly on the radio.

The boys followed Nojo a short distance into the hallway at the back of the control room, where he stopped and waved his hand. The door to the bridge closed behind them and sealed. They heard a hissing sound as the air was sucked out. Finally, the floor in front of them tilted down and turned into the boarding ramp. When it was all the way down, they strolled down the ramp and out, into the vast alien hangar.

15. The Delphian's Door

"Remember boys," cautioned Nojo as they stepped onto the floor of the giant hangar, "we've left the artificial gravity of the ship and the gravity here on the moon is only one-fifth as strong as it is on Earth. So, be careful, you'll be much stronger here on the moon than you were on Earth."

"Oh yeah, I saw that on TV," said Jake. "The Apollo astronauts used to bounce around instead of walking."

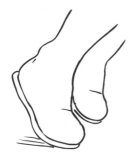

Scott decided to give it a try and jumped up. He launched off the floor, went right over Jake's head, and landed gently, just like he was Superman. "Yes!" shouted Scott, pumping his fist up and down.

"I'm going to try a back flip," announced Jake. He shot up like a spring and somersaulted backwards high above Scott and Nojo's heads, then landed square on his feet just like

he'd done it a zillion times before. "Sweet!" he cried. "This is better than a trampoline."

"You two can do gymnastics all the way to the door if you want. It's this way," Nojo announced, and he started bounding in long, graceful leaps toward the hallway entrance.

Jake and Scott followed him playing leapfrog, each one yelling, "Ready, set, rocket ship," then vaulting high in the air and landing with great fanfare after their flight. They did twists and turns in mid-vault, each leap more elaborate than the last. A short way down the hall Nojo stopped in front of a large door and the two boys bounded up next to him.

"This is it," said Nojo, "the door that I couldn't open without the key from Earth. Now you two are the key, so you'll have to open it."

"But we don't know how," protested Scott.

"See that circular spot?" said Nojo, pointing to a bowl-shaped depression in the door. "That's where the spherical key would have fit. I think if you two touch there, the door just might open."

The boys looked at each other and simultaneously said, "Okay." They stood on opposite sides of the hole, each holding their hands next to each other they did a count-down together. "Three, two, one, touch." When they touched the key-hole, a tingle went up their arms and funny symbols flashed through their minds, but only for an instant.

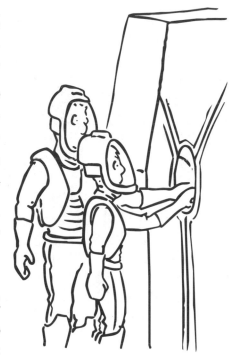

Three ticks of a clock later the door slid open, revealing an entrance chamber beyond the door. Unlike the landing pad, which was practically bare, this chamber was filled with round pictures on the walls and statues on the sides. They stepped into the chamber and could see that it was more like a wide hallway than a room. It appeared to be carved right from glowing moon rock. The hall went straight for a few yards then turned a corner a little way down.

The pictures and the statues were fascinating. Some of the pictures were of strange buildings in faraway worlds and some were of people, but not

like any people Jake or Scott had ever seen. The people all had faces like birds, but bodies that looked almost human, except for the downy feathers covering them. There were large vases on the floor with scenes of other worlds painted on the sides, and two large statues of the bird people standing on opposite sides of the hall. The statues had sharp hawk bills where their noses should have been, and each one held a long staff in its hand.

"These must be the Delphians," said Jake looking closely at one of the strange round paintings.

"You're absolutely right," said Nojo examining some

66

inscriptions written on the wall. "The Delphians looked similar to birds on your world. They're a rather handsome people, really."

"I'm going to check out the stuff down there," announced Scott, starting towards some large purple vases at the other end of the hall.

"Don't go far—we'll try to find the waypoint as soon as I translate a few of these messages," Nojo replied, peering at the strange Delphian writing 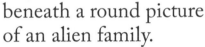 beneath a round picture of an alien family.

Scott barely looked at the large statues of the Delphians as he passed them. If he had taken a moment to look closer, he might have noticed that their dark lifeless eyes suddenly opened and followed him as he strolled past to examine the ancient alien relics at the end of the hall.

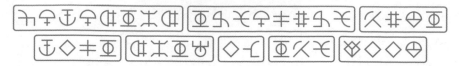

⛭⛭⛭⛭⛭⛭⛭⛭ ⛭⛭⛭⛭⛭⛭⛭⛭ ⛭⛭⛭⛭

⛭⛭⛭⛭ ⛭⛭⛭⛭ ⛭⛭ ⛭⛭⛭ ⛭⛭⛭⛭

⛭⛭⛭⛭⛭⛭

16. The Guards Awake

A slight shudder shook the floor of the room as the two statues lifted their staffs and struck them on the ground. The tips of the staffs started to open up like a flower just starting to bloom. Four metal petals around the central shaft sparkled and glowed with little bits of lightning that trickled out of the petals and arched in flickers toward a wicked point at the end. The statues were opening their beaks and seemed to be speaking, but they couldn't be heard in the airless room. Then both of them stepped out into the hall and turned toward

Scott, who was bounding along, still unaware that the statues had come to life. Nojo and Jake had seen them though. They had watched them awaken in silent awe.

"Oh dear," said Nojo, "they must be robot guards. We've got to get back to the ship."

"I'm not sure they're going to let us," said Jake, seeing the guards point their staffs towards the ceiling above Scott.

"Scott, look out!" yelled Jake over the radio, his voice echoing inside his helmet.

Scott turned around to see what was going on, just as a bolt of lightning shot out of one of the guardbot's staffs. The electric arc hit the ceiling and sparks flew down like Fourth of July fireworks. He instinctively dove for cover behind one of the purple vases on the side of the hallway before the guard could fire another shot.

"That was just a warning shot," said Nojo breathlessly, "but they might mean business next time, so we've got to get Scott out of there."

"Shoot the robots with a laser or something, quick!" barked Jake.

"I didn't bring any weapons. I wasn't expecting anything like this," replied Nojo. "We'll just have to distract them."

The Delphian robots were starting to aim their staffs toward the vase where Scott had hidden, and hadn't seemed to notice Jake or Nojo yet. Jake was frantic to distract them and was looking for something to throw. He saw that the circular paintings on the wall were made from some kind of metal and had an idea.

"Throw the paintings!" yelled Jake. He grabbed two paintings off the wall, one in each hand. He threw the first one like a Frisbee, aiming at the guard on the right, hitting it in the back of the head. Before the first guard could even turn, Jake hurled the second disk as hard as he could. It was a perfect backhand toss, striking the second guard's staff just as it was about to discharge a lightning bolt. The metal disk exploded in a fireball of electricity, momentarily blinding the robot guards.

"Great throw, Jake!" congratulated Nojo. "Come on, let's get past them while they're distracted."

"You go now, while I keep them busy. I'll be along in a second," replied Jake. Then he called out to Scott, "Hang tough buddy, we're comin'!"

Jake grabbed two more of the paintings off the wall, while keeping an eye on Nojo, who was racing to get past the guards. The guard-bots were turning towards him and their eyes flashed red in warning. Jake threw a disk with expert aim. It skipped off the far wall and ricocheted towards the robots' heads. They both raised their staffs toward

it and fired, just as Nojo approached. Nojo kept low and slipped past them, even as the shower of sparks from the exploding metal painting rained down all around him.

Jake tossed the last disk, skipping it off the ground in front of him as he ran in huge leaps at the guardbots. The disk flew at the robots' legs, distracting them just enough. With a final mighty leap, Jake used the low gravity to jump high up on the side of the hall, then he bounced off the wall in a somersault over the bird-like machines. It was the ultimate game of leapfrog. Jake pushed on the head of a guard as he passed and sent the robot sprawling to the ground.

Jake landed right beside

Nojo and Scott, tucking into a quick roll to stop himself behind the vases. Then he jumped up and shouted, "Come on, we've got to get out while one of them is down."

"It's too late," said Nojo quickly, "it's already getting up."

The fallen guard-bot was starting to stand, and the second guard-bot pointed his staff straight at them.

17. Escape from the Delphian Guards

The guards started walking toward them, their staffs buzzing with electricity. The Delphian guards were getting ready to let fly with more lightning.

"We'll have to make a run for it and then try to find another way out," said Nojo. "You boys go first; don't let me slow you down."

"You don't have to tell me twice! I'm out of here," announced Scott, bolting for where the hall turned the corner just a few feet away.

Jake and Nojo were right behind Scott, and none too soon. A blast of lightning lit up the chamber with a brilliant flash. The vases they were hiding behind vaporized and a spray of pottery fragments shot in all directions.

"Yowza, that was close!" yelped Jake, as they rounded the corner of the hall, and were out of the range of the lightning sticks.

Just a little way down the hall was a round-walled side passage that sloped steeply downward. Jake stopped and looked briefly down the incline, then up at the round paintings on the walls. "Hey wait guys, I've got an idea," he said, while he pulled a huge saucer-shaped picture off the wall and tossed it on the floor.

"I hope it's a fast idea, because here come the robots," announced Scott, pointing back down the hall at the guards marching after them.

"We'll use the paintings like sleds," said Jake. "You two ride on this one and I'll get another."

"That's brilliant!" exclaimed Nojo, pushing the sled to the edge of the slope while Scott climbed into the front. Nojo climbed onto the back of their sled and gave a last push to start them down the stone ramp.

Jake grabbed a smaller oval painting off the wall, threw it to the ground and jumped on, still standing, riding it like a snowboard. The low gravity caused the disk to bounce up with every bump. It almost

felt like he
was flying down the
tunnel. The board would touch
down for a moment and then skip back upward
into a long, graceful arc. Jake let out a "Yeehaw!"
as he shot down the tunnel right behind Scott and
Nojo, sparks flying from the bottom of their metal
disks.

After a bit, the tunnel turned sharply to the right.
The sleds rode up the walls, like they were shooting a half-pipe at a skate park. Jake weaved his
board back and forth
jumping over ob-
stacles in his
way, touching
down only
briefly be-
tween skips.
The tunnel
twisted and
turned, first
right, then left
and then right
again. Each time,

they'd
ride their disks up
the walls and back down. On
one steep turn Jake even rode his board up
over the top of the tunnel and down the other wall
in a loop-de-loop. "Yes," he shouted with glee. "This
is an outrageous ride!"

As they descended below the surface of the moon, they started noticing a pulsing blue light shining up the tunnel from further ahead. The deeper they went, the brighter it got. The tunnel made a last turn to the left. Just ahead, the tunnel flattened out briefly, and beyond the flat spot they could see that the pulsing light was coming from an enormous machine in the center of a cavern. Suddenly they realized that the tunnel had ended. It didn't end in a wall. It ended in nothing. They were rapidly approaching a giant cliff at the edge of the cavern... and they were going much too fast to stop.

⟦ 𖤐⟧

18. Free Fall

"Jake, jump onto our sled," commanded Nojo firmly.

Without any hesitation, Jake skidded his board toward the sled in the last few feet before the cliff, and jumped for it, just as they all sailed off into nothingness. He landed between Scott and Nojo and grabbed on. The saucer rocked wildly when Jake hit and threatened to flip over, but some quick weight-shifting by Scott got it back under control.

The saucer, with all three of them on it, was falling to the cavern floor far below while still moving forward, just like they'd gone off a ski jump. Because of the moon's low gravity, they weren't free-falling too fast just yet, but they were starting to pick up speed, and it was a long way down.

"What do we do now?" cried Scott.

Nojo pulled his wand out of his belt pouch. "I don't think the wand has enough power to actually lift us," he said touching the wand to the metal edge of the sled. "But, its anti-gravity field just might be able to slow us down."

They held their breath for a moment, watching the ground approaching at frightening speed. "The anti-gravity is working," called Jake, "we're starting to slow down."

"It's working all right, but it's still going to be a rough landing," said Nojo. "Hold on!"

The sled slammed into the ground in a hard skid, with sparks flying. They tumbled out onto the ground, but they were all right. They picked them-

selves up slowly, each amazed to be in one piece. All three of them were pumped up from the excitement of the chase and the crash. Now that it was over and they weren't hurt, it seemed like a grand adventure.

"That was a radical ride, Nojo," said Jake holding his palm in a high five. "Nice move with the wand."

Nojo slapped Jake's hand, and then offered a high five to Scott. "We would have been goners if Scott hadn't been quick to steady the sled. I'd say, congratulations all around."

Scott slapped his hand hard. "Yeah baby!" he whooped.

Nojo put his wand away and looked at the pulsing machine in front of him. Tubes and ducts went in all directions from a central sphere that gave off the eerie glow. "This must be the energy source that's powered this place for thousands of years. I'll bet we're in the heart of the city."

"At least we gave those robots the slip," said Jake. "Now we just have to find a way out of here."

"Look, there's a passage over there," announced Scott, who was pointing to a tunnel entrance in the cavern wall on the right.

No sooner had he spoken than a blast of lightning struck the ground a few feet to their left. They looked up, and there on the rim of the cliff high above were the two hawk-faced robots.

"Run for the tunnel," said Nojo as a second lightning bolt struck the ground.

All three of them bounded for the passageway as fast as they could while lightning bolts exploded around them.

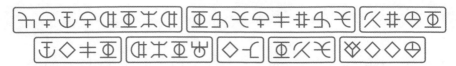

19. Waypoint to the Pillar of Knowledge

They made it in just a handful of giant leaps and ducked safely into the entrance. Lightning bolts struck the ground outside the doorway, lighting up the tunnel in brilliant but harmless flashes.

"I guess those guys just don't know when to quit," remarked Jake.

"You're right about that," said Nojo. "Let's get back to the ship before they find us again."

Scott looked down the corridor and saw that there were a couple of side passages just ahead. "Which way should we go?"

Nojo pulled the wand out of his pouch and swung it in a circle. It pulsed with a rainbow of lights and let out a strange warbling sound that Nojo seemed to understand. After a few moments, a big frog-grin spread across his face. "The ship should be just up that passage on the right. But we might want take a short detour," he said pausing for a second, both his transparent eyelids blinking in excitement, "because I'm pretty sure that just down the one to our left is where we'll find the waypoint to the Pillar of Knowledge."

"Let's do it," said Scott already bouncing toward the tunnel on the left.

The passage was very short, only a few yards long. At the end of it was a door, very much like the one that they had opened to get into the lost city in the first place. It had more strange writing on it and another circular keyhole designed to hold the spherical key.

Without any prompting from Nojo, Scott and Jake bounded up to the key hole. "Same as last time, okay?" said Jake, and Scott nodded in agreement.

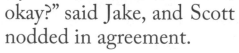

Jake did the countdown. "Three, two, one, touch," and the two boys touched the center knob. Once again alien symbols flashed before their eyes, and obediently, the door opened.

Beyond was a room, not much bigger than an elevator, with a single object floating in the center of the room. It was a small four-sided pyramid, about the size of a traffic cone, sitting on a round silver plate that hovered a few feet above the floor. The pyramid was jet-black, more than jet-black really; it was so black that it seemed to be sucking the very light out of the room. Although it was clearly a pyramid shape, it

was difficult to tell if it had a solid surface or was some kind of strange hole.

Nojo approached the waypoint to the Pillar of Knowledge cautiously, his wand in front of him. The wand warbled frantically and pulsed brighter than the boys had ever seen. "Fascinating," said Nojo with a bit of awe in his voice. "These readings indicate that it's not really an object at all, but more like a frozen chunk of space-time."

"Okay," said Jake, "you've got me on this one. What the heck is space-time?"

"Space-time is what the universe is made of. Everything is made of space-time, even atoms," said Nojo. "In normal

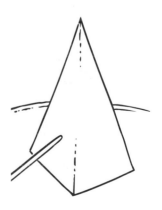

85

space-time, time is always moving forward like a clock, but in this pyramid, time is frozen. This is a frozen piece of time from very long ago."

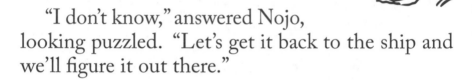

"That's very weird. So, where does it say the Pillar of Knowledge is?" asked Scott anxiously.

"I don't know," answered Nojo, looking puzzled. "Let's get it back to the ship and we'll figure it out there."

Nojo grabbed the floating silver plate easy as you please, and headed back down the hall carrying the black pyramid as if it were a birthday cake on a platter. They went back into the main hall and then headed for the passage on the right, back to the ship.

Just as they approached the side passage to the

surface Jake glanced down the tunnel into the cavern. What he saw froze him in his tracks. The two guard-bots had just appeared on the far side of the gigantic power generator. The hawk-faced hunters were running straight for them at incredible speed, making giant fifty-foot leaps across the huge open space. They would be across the cavern and inside the tunnel in a few moments.

"Robots!" shouted Jake. "Run!"

20. Return of the Robots

The three of them raced into the passage with their hearts thumping. The tunnel was curving slightly to the left and started to slope up, which was encouraging. Suddenly, they came to a fork in the tunnel and they all stopped.

"Which way Nojo, left or right?" asked Scott breathlessly, eyeing the two tunnels, both of which sloped upward.

"I'm not sure," confessed Nojo. "The ship should be dead ahead, but I don't have a map, so I don't know which tunnel will take us there. I guess we'll just have to pick one and hope for the best."

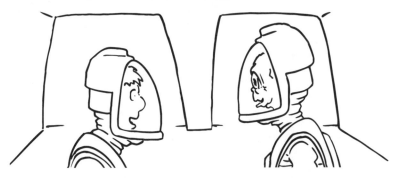

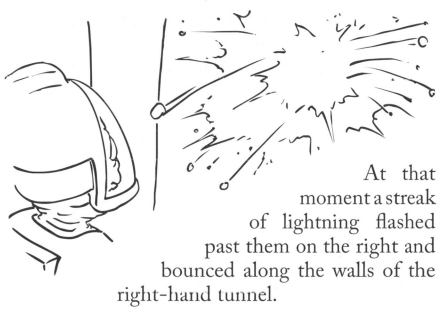

At that moment a streak of lightning flashed past them on the right and bounced along the walls of the right-hand tunnel.

"Left!" yelled Nojo, leaping into the left-hand passage.

"Yowza, that was close!" exclaimed Jake as he ran, bringing up the rear behind Nojo and Scott. "We're never gonna ditch these guys. We've gotta take 'em out."

A few moments later they emerged into a large circular room, the size of a basketball court, with a high ceiling to match. It might once have been some kind of meeting hall, because it was essentially empty, except high up on the walls there were more of the giant round metal paintings. They looked like portraits, and could have been leaders of the long lost Delphian civilization. There were half a dozen passages leading out of the room, but none of them had a big neon sign over it saying, "THIS WAY TO YOUR STARSHIP".

"What now?" asked Scott looking to Nojo.

But before Nojo could answer, Jake spoke up. "I've got an idea," he said, looking up at the very large painted shield over the tunnel they'd just

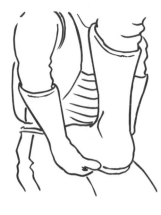

emerged from. "Let's drop that painting on those robots. That'll shut 'em down."

Nojo looked up the wall at the painting, on a small ledge thirty feet above the floor. "That's a long way up, Jake. It would be a mighty leap, even for you."

"I could do it," exclaimed Scott excitedly. "If Jake throws me just as I jump, I bet I could reach it. Dad does it with us at the pool." Scott nodded his head at Jake, who nodded back. "You know I can reach it."

"All right, buddy. Saddle up quick—we don't have much time," said Jake squatting down and holding his hands low for Scott to step into.

Scott put both his feet in Jake's hands and coiled his legs for a big push.

"Ready, set,
ROCKET-SHIP!"
they yelled in unison.

Jake pushed off the floor
with his feet and threw with
his arms. At the same time
Scott jumped as hard as he
could. He flew like Superman,
his arms outstretched in front
of him. The low
gravity of the
moon almost
made the
incredible
leap seem
easy. Scott
sailed up to
the ledge
and gently
landed on

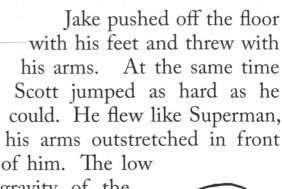

92

both feet just like a gymnast who'd done it a hundred times before.

"Yeah baby, nice job!" shouted Jake, making a small jump of joy himself.

Jake's joy lasted but a second, since a heartbeat later the robots emerged from the tunnel. Electricity flickered at the tips of their staffs and they pointed them menacingly at Jake and Nojo just a few feet away. Nojo held the black pyramid in front of him defiantly and Jake slowly raised his hands over his head, hoping that the guards wouldn't shoot.

21. Robot Revenge

"Eat this, beak face!" shouted Scott, tipping the giant metal shield off its perch. It tumbled off the ledge in slow motion, the moon's gravity accelerating it weakly. At first it fell slowly, then a little faster, then faster still.

Jake watched the heavy disk gathering speed, hurtling downward toward the robots. He hoped it would get there before he and Nojo were vaporized by a bolt of lightning.

The robots paid no attention to the falling shield. They were standing frozen in place, staring at the pyramid held in Nojo's hands, when the impact came. The guard-bots were knocked to the ground in an instant, their lightning staffs scattering across the floor. The metal painting was so large it nearly covered them both and pinned them to the ground, their arms and legs splayed out all catty-wompus.

"Sweet shot!" yelled Jake, completely jazzed.

Scott was doing a little dance on the ledge, singing, "We are the champions! We are the champions!"

Nojo nodded at the boy as he sang and danced, "Very well done young man. You've got a spot on my bowling team any day."

Then Nojo shifted the waypoint pyramid so he could hold it with one hand and pull out his wand with the other. "Jump and I'll slow you down with the wand," he shouted up to Scott.

Scott looked down with a bit of concern on his face; it was a long way to jump, even on the moon. It was like looking down from the top of a three-story building. After a moment's hesitation, Scott screwed up his courage, yelled "Geronimo!"

and leapt. His arms flailed as he tried to keep his balance as he fell. Nojo's wand slowed him to a leisurely descent and he landed soft as a cat on carpet. "Hey, that was almost fun," he said, relieved to be on the ground.

"The eagle has landed," chirped Jake, proud of how brave his little brother had been.

Nojo put his wand away and was trying to figure out which tunnel to take when the robots started to stir under the shield. "Come on boys, those guards aren't out of the game yet. Let's try the tunnel over there." He nodded toward the entrance opposite them and started moving that way.

No sooner had they entered the new tunnel, when they saw two new beak-faced guards coming toward them from deeper in the passageway. "Oh dear," said Nojo, "there're more of the ruddy things. Quick, another tunnel."

All three spun around, raced out of the tunnel and bounded for the passage to the right. It was no use; Delphian guard-bots were coming down that tunnel as well. They went for the next entrance in line. Before they even got halfway there, three menacing guards emerged from the opening they were sprinting toward, their staffs at the ready.

The boys and Nojo stopped in their tracks and looked for an escape, but from every tunnel guards were entering the chamber. The three of them stayed clustered together and slowly backed into the center of the room. More than a dozen robots surrounded them. The bots advanced slowly, while blue fingers of electricity waved at the tips of their staffs.

"This is not good," said Jake matter-of-factly.

22. The Waypoint Rules

"All right lads, we're not done for yet," said Nojo, trying to sound more hopeful than he felt. "Maybe they just want a little chat."

Jake looked at the ever-tightening circle of Delphian bots. Ominous red lights blinked slowly in their robot eyes. "I don't think they want to chat, dude," he said. "I think they're planning a weenie roast, and we're the weenies."

"A gravity field around us just might deflect a lightning bolt," said Nojo without much conviction. "At least it's worth a try. Take the waypoint, boys, and I'll get out my wand."

Nojo thrust the platter with the waypoint on it toward Jake and Scott. They each grabbed one side of the silver disk. The second that they both touched it, symbols flashed to life in a rainbow of colors on the silver tray. Then the deep black pyramid itself started to change. Tiny points of light appeared

inside the inky faces of its shape and began to grow brighter and more numerous with each passing second. Light streamed out of the waypoint, casting a glow over their faces.

All three of them stood spellbound. As Nojo and the boys gazed into the pyramid, they suddenly realized they were looking at stars, planets, and moons. Not just a movie or picture of the heavens, but miniature versions of entire solar systems and other worlds captured in the waypoint. It was the most beautiful thing they had ever seen.

Nojo finally tore his eyes away from the sight, determined to put up a last-ditch defense with his wand. He glanced at the robots and then announced rather smugly, "I told you we weren't done for. I love it when I'm right."

Jake and Scott looked up from the stars and saw all of the Delphian robots kneeling around them. The beaked heads were lowered, and their blasters lay on the ground. It was the second most beautiful thing they'd ever seen.

"What happened?" asked Jake in disbelief.

"I should have thought of it sooner," replied Nojo chastising himself. "You boys are the key keepers, the waypoint turned on when you touched it. Looks to me like the waypoint rules these robots. Since you turned the waypoint on, I'm guessing that you are now the masters of our new friends."

"Wooow, I can't wait till the guys hear about this," said Scott. "Can we take a couple of them home with us?"

Nojo shook his head slowly, "I'm not sure that's such a great idea. If they blasted somebody you'd get in a lot of trouble. However, we might want to ask them to lead us back to the ship."

"Okay, that sounds like a plan," said Jake pondering the thought, "but how do we talk to them? Do you speak Delphian?"

"I don't speak it, but I do write it," replied Nojo, whipping out his wand. He waved it gently and symbols from a strange alphabet appeared, floating between them and the nearest guards.

The robots responded by immediately forming an honor guard on each side of them with one guard-bot in the lead. When they were all in their positions, the column started up a tunnel that led to the ship.

"Now this is more like it," said Jake with a smile on his face.

23. Back to the Beginning

Upon their arrival at the ship, the robots carefully arranged themselves for a formal send-off. The guards stood at attention on each side of the boarding ramp, each one bowing in turn as Nojo and the boys bounded past them into the spacecraft. Once aboard, Nojo closed the ramp and pressurized the airlock so they could enter the bridge and take off their space suits.

Scott was quietly humming "We are the Champions" as he took off his space suit and tossed it on the bridge deck.

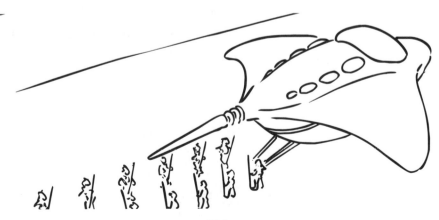

Jake finished peeling off his own suit and was staring at the tiny solar systems with their suns shining within the waypoint that floated above a side table. "So, now that it's turned on, where does this thingy say the Pillar of Knowledge is?"

"Good question," answered Nojo, sitting down in his control chair and preparing to take off. "It's clearly a map of some kind. The one thing I have discovered so far is that it's not just a map of stars and planets, but a map of time as well. It will take some study to understand it, but that will have to wait. I should get you boys back home."

Jake thought about going home for a second, and then suddenly looked startled, his eyes growing wide. "Oh no, we're dead meat," he said with a groan. "We've been gone for hours. Our folks are going to kill us!"

"Don't worry. It's still the middle of the night at your house, Jake, and I'll have you back in a jiffy," said Nojo calmly as he expertly guided them out of the lost city and into moon orbit.

"You don't know my mom, Nojo," said Jake, sounding defeated. "No way would she go to bed without checking on us in the backyard. She's probably got the whole town looking for us by now."

"We'll be grounded for the rest of our lives!" wailed Scott, realizing his brother was right.

"No problem. We'll just have to go back in time then, won't we?" said Nojo, wearing his sly smile.

"You have a time machine?!" said Jake, not sure whether to be impressed or doubtful.

"Not exactly," replied Nojo banking the ship left toward an empty patch of space. "But I do know where I can find one. It's a wormhole that the Delphians built here in lunar orbit."

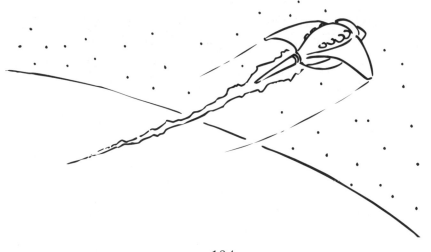

"Okaaay, you got me again Nojo. What's a wormhole?" asked Jake.

"Well, it's sort of a hole in the fabric of space and time. In fact it's right in front of us now," Nojo said, pointing to a particularly black and empty patch of the star-scape in front of them. "The normal laws of space and time do not apply inside the wormhole. If you know exactly where to enter it and where to exit it, you can go anywhere in time that you wish. It's sort of like taking the correct off-ramp from a freeway."

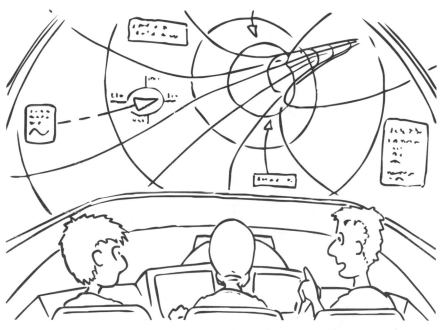

"You mean we fly into that thing and come out back in time?" responded Jake in disbelief.

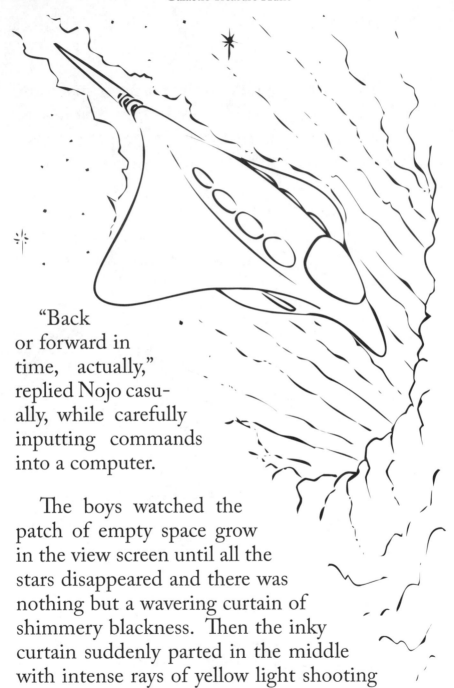

"Back
or forward in
time, actually,"
replied Nojo casu-
ally, while carefully
inputting commands
into a computer.

The boys watched the
patch of empty space grow
in the view screen until all the
stars disappeared and there was
nothing but a wavering curtain of
shimmery blackness. Then the inky
curtain suddenly parted in the middle
with intense rays of yellow light shooting

out of the center. As the ship fell ever faster, it changed colors from yellow through blue to blinding white. At the same moment, a deep humming sound erupted. For a moment the boys had the strange sensation that millions of people surrounded them, all singing the same note.

"All right then, get ready boys! We're going back in time!" shouted Nojo, above the singing of the wormhole.

24. Home Again

When they exited the wormhole nothing looked any different. The stars were the same, the moon was the same, and their town looked the same as they approached from space. Everything was just as they'd left it.

"Are you sure we went back in time?" asked Scott. "I don't feel any different."

"Oh, I'm quite sure," said Nojo with authority. "In fact, if my calculations are correct, we should be arriving over your house right about the same time as we all blasted off from the forest a few hours ago. Ah yes, there we are," he said with triumph, pointing to their star ship as it zoomed away right in front of them.

"Oh man, too weird," said Jake, looking at himself in the front window of the other ship as it took off for the moon.

Nojo landed the ship in the same clearing as before, lowered the ramp and walked the boys back into the forest. "I can't tell you how wonderful it has been to meet you," he said in a very serious voice. "I've never met two braver or smarter boys. Now before you go, I've got something for each of you." Nojo pulled a little metallic ball from his pouch, twisted it in half and then handed one half to each boy. "These are two halves of a little radio," he told them. "When you want to talk to me, just put them back together and say my name. I'll hear you wherever I am."

Scott and Jake each took their piece of the radio and nodded slowly, sad that their adventure had ended, and knowing that they would miss Nojo.

"Will we see you again?" asked Scott hopefully, as Nojo gave each of them a good-bye hug.

"I sure hope so," said Nojo with a smile and a wink of a transparent eyelid. "Now, get on with ya. We don't want your mom to find you gone."

25. We Really Did Go to the Moon

The next morning Jake and Scott woke up in the backyard still tingling with the excitement of the night before. They walked into the kitchen where Dad was reading the Saturday newspaper and Mom was making pancakes, just like every other Saturday morning they could remember.

"Hey guys," called their dad, putting the paper down. "How was your campout?"

"Uhhh… it was cool," said Jake, looking at Scott and making a motion like he was going to zap him with an imaginary lightning bolt.

Scott laughed and pretended to shoot him back. "Yeah, it was really cool! We met this space alien, who like landed in the back yard, and then we went to the moon, and then we battled with these robots that looked like birds, and then we went through a wormhole that sounded like the choir at church, but not exactly like the choir, because it didn't have Mr. Wilson making that funny honking sound he always makes," he said breathlessly. Then he added as an afterthought, "And Jake got to drive the space-ship, but I didn't get to, but I might get to in about a hundred years."

"That sounds like a very exciting campout," said their mom casually, not even looking up from the pancake she was flipping. "I hope you dressed warmly on the moon."

"I told you they wouldn't believe us," Jake whispered to Scott, as they sat down for breakfast.

"I heard something almost as wild as that," their dad said, putting some toast on their plates. "I saw coach Johnson this morning. He said some pranksters painted a crazy maze on the soccer field

111

last night. He thinks it was the Wilson twins, but maybe...," his voice shifted to a monster growl "it was a space alien! Wahaha!"

The two boys looked at each other and burst out laughing.

Several days later it seemed like the whole thing had never happened. If it weren't for the little metal half-spheres they carried, they'd have been starting to wonder if it was all just a dream. They'd talked about calling Nojo dozens of times, but they didn't want to seem like pests. After all, he was a busy archeologist and everything. Then, one day as they were playing catch in the back yard, a humming started coming from their pockets. They each pulled out their half of the radio and put them together.

Nojo's voice came out of it at once. "Hey-ho lads, how's your summer?"

"Aaah, just fine, Nojo. How about you?" replied Jake, thrilled to hear from the little alien.

"Good, good," said Nojo quickly. "I missed you boys though, and I think I've figured out the way-point. I don't suppose you're up for another trip are you?" he inquired.

"Are you kidding?" they responded in unison. "Yeaahh!"

"Where are we going?" asked Scott, all excited.

"Well, that's the tricky part isn't it," replied Nojo. "It's not so much a where, as it is a when. We're going back in time... way back."

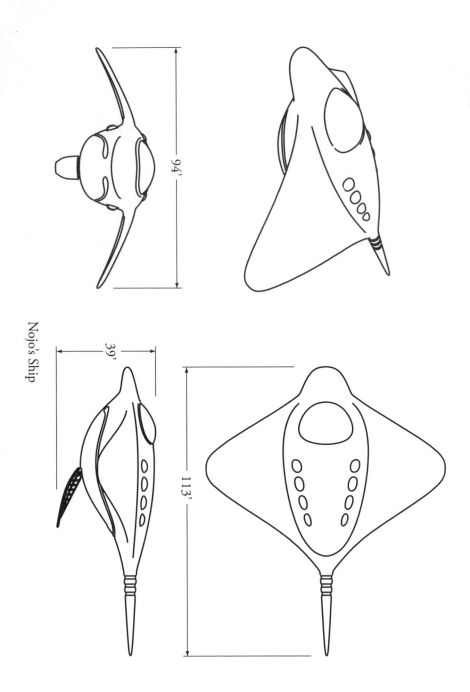

Nojo's Ship

94'

39'

113'

If you want to find out where Jake and Scott are going on their next exciting adventure with Nojo, copy the Delphian words found at the beginning of each chapter and write them down in order.

Fortunately for you, Nojo was kind enough to leave a copy of the Delphian alphabet decoder.

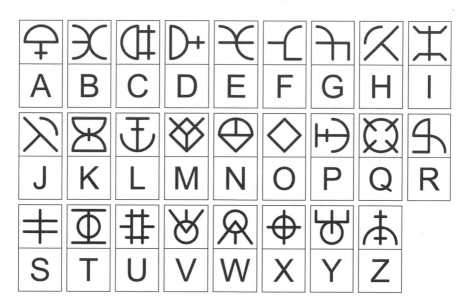